THE SMALL POT~~ATOES~~ AND THE SNOWBALL FIGHT

Harriet Ziefert

Illustrated by Richard Brown

A Yearling Book

Published by
Dell Publishing Co., Inc.
1 Dag Hammarskjold Plaza
New York, New York 10017

Yearling ® TM 913705, Dell Publishing Co., Inc.

ISBN: 0-440-48115-5

Printed in the United States of America

July 1986

10 9 8 7 6 5 4 3 2

CW

For my nephew, Sam

CHAPTER ONE

IT'S SNOWING

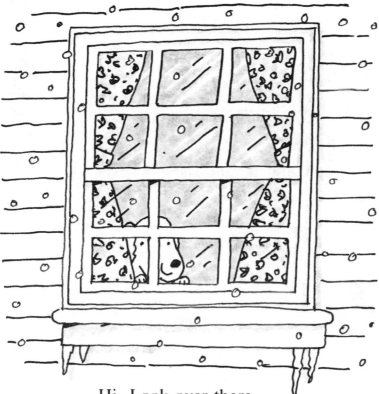

Hi. Look over there.

That's Molly's house.

And look in the window.

Upstairs, behind the curtains,

is her dog, Spot.

Spot woke Molly early.

"Arf! Arf!" he barked.

"It's snowing!"

Molly jumped out of bed and
ran to the window.

The snow looked perfect and already
there was a lot of it.

Molly thought of snowballs, and snowmen,
and snow angels, and snow cones.

Molly turned to Spot and said, "We're going
to have a good time today. But I'd better
call Roger. The more kids we get, the more
fun we'll have."

Molly dialed Roger's phone number.

The phone rang five times before Roger
picked up the receiver.

He must have been sleeping.

"Hi, Roger," said Molly. "Do you know
it's been snowing all night?"

"Wait a minute," Roger answered. "I have
    to put on my glasses."
"Why do you need eyeglasses to talk to me?"
    Molly asked.
"Because I can't think straight without them,"
    Roger answered.
  Soon Roger came back on the line.
"I saw the snow!" he shouted. "It's super."
"Do you want to play in it later?" Molly asked.
"Yup," Roger answered. "But I know I'll have
    to wear boots and snow pants."

"Me too," Molly said.

"Should we call a *Small Potatoes* meeting?"
    Roger asked.

"I think so," said Molly. "Let's have a meeting
    at ten o'clock in the park. Near the duck pond."

Roger said he would call Sam and Chris.

Molly said she would call Sue and Scott.

"See ya at the meeting," Roger said.

"Bye, see ya," Molly said as she hung up
    the phone.

Sam got to the park first.

His ski cap came down to his eyebrows.

His scarf was wrapped around his mouth and chin.

Only his eyes and nose were showing.

And his freckles too.

Sue came with Molly and Spot.

Her braids hung down from under her hat.

Sue's braids weren't frozen yet,

but they probably would be later.

Chris wore his ski clothes and baseball hat.
Chris always wore his baseball hat—
even in winter.
But in the snow he also put on earmuffs.
Scott came last.
By himself.
He looked unhappy.
He said he hated being
all bundled up in winter clothes.
In boots and snow pants.
And he hated wearing mittens, and a scarf,
and a hat.

"So we're all here," said Molly.

"Who's starting the meeting?"

"I will," said Roger. "Is there any old business?"

"It's been a long time since the last meeting,"
said Chris. "I can't remember anything."

"New business?" Roger asked.

"I think the new business should be about what
to do in the snow," said Molly.

"I agree," said Scott. "We'd better think of
something to do—fast!"

"Before we freeze!" added Chris.

"Why don't we build a winter clubhouse?"
yelled Sam.

"Yeah," agreed Roger. "We could use one."

"But how?" Chris asked.

"I'm sure we could figure out something—like a
cave," Sam said.

"Or an igloo," Sue said.

"Should we vote?" Roger asked.

"It's too cold," said Sam. "Let's just start."

Sam found a big snowdrift.

He asked Molly and Chris to help him dig.

Maybe they could carve out a doorway.

Or even a little room.

Maybe.

Whatever they made, it would be the start

of something good.

CHAPTER TWO

CAVE? OR IGLOO?

"You can't make an igloo," said Scott.

"Oh, you're just in a bad mood," said Molly.

"I am in a bad mood," Scott answered. "But
I also know it can't be done."

"How do you know?" asked Chris.

"I know because I read a book about how
     Eskimos build igloos," said Scott.

"What did it say?" asked Roger.

"It said that the snow must be twenty inches
     deep and packed firmly or it will not make
     strong blocks for building."

"This snow is less than a foot," said Sue.

"And it also said Eskimos cut snow blocks with
     snow knives—more than one hundred blocks—
     to make one igloo!"

"We can't do that! No way!" Roger said.

"But we can dig!" shouted Molly from where she was working.

"*Arf! Arf!*" barked Spot, who wanted everyone to know he could dig too.

"If we all dig," said Sam, "we can make a tunnel."

"I'll help," Roger said.

"So will I," added Sue.

"I'll help too," grumbled Scott. "As long as you know you're not making an igloo!"

"Yeah. We know it. But we're having fun anyway," Molly said.

After much digging, there was a doorway.

It looked something like the doorway of an igloo.

Because everybody kept working, the doorway grew deeper.

Soon, there was a tunnel.

It was big enough for Molly, Roger, and Sue.

And Spot too!

16

"If we just dig a little harder," said Sam, "this
tunnel will be something like a cave. And all
of us will fit inside."

"Can we rest then?" asked Chris, who was getting
tired of digging.

"Sure, we can," said Roger. "But no resting yet."

"How much more?" Scott asked.

"Not much," answered Molly. "When we're
done, I have a surprise."

"What is it?" Scott asked.

"I'm not telling," said Molly. "You guess."

"Is it food?" Sue asked.

"Sort of," Molly answered.

"Where is it?" Scott asked.

"In my pocket," Molly answered.

"Well, it can't be very much—if it fits in
your pocket," Scott grumped.

"It's more than you think," snapped Molly, who
was getting upset by Scott's bad mood.

"Let's see if we can all fit into this tunnel,"
said Roger.
Roger, Sam, Chris,
Molly, Sue, and Scott
crawled into the tunnel.
And so did Spot.
"We all fit!"
"We're done!"
"Hooray!"

"Molly, can we have your surprise now?"
    Sue asked.

"Okay," said Molly as she reached into her pocket.

Molly pulled out four packets of Kool-Aid.

Lime-green, grape-purple, cherry-red, and
lemon-yellow.

"We can make snow cones," Molly announced
    with a big smile.

Spot smiled too.

He knew Molly would give him a lick, or
maybe even his own cone.

Molly continued. "I'll show you how to do it.

    First, we have to find absolutely clean snow."

"Absolutely clean?" Sam said.

"Right," answered Molly. "That's why the only time to make snow cones is now. Right after the snow stops."

"Before people walk on it," Roger said.

"And before dogs make yellow spots on it," Chris added.

"So find yourself a handful of pure, snow-white snow," Molly said. "Then bring it to me and I'll sprinkle on some flavoring."

Roger and Sue wanted cherry.

Chris and Sam wanted grape.

Scott couldn't make up his mind.

He watched Molly pour green powder

onto her handful of snow.

It was a beautiful color green.

So Scott took lime.

"Give me some more cherry," said Sue.

"I licked all my flavor off the top."

"I'll take some lemon-yellow," said Roger.

"Maybe my cherry cone will turn orange!"

"It will," said Molly. "Just watch!"

Molly sprinkled lemon powder onto Roger's snow.

Then everybody watched Molly as she mixed

other beautiful colors in the snow.

"From red, yellow, and blue, you can make

everything," she said.

CHAPTER THREE

SNOWBALLS

"Let's play a game," said Sue. "Let's think
of words that start with *snow*."

Someone said *snowstorm*.

Then *snowdrift* and *snowbank*.

Snowplow too.

Roger said, "*Snowshoe*—my father
    has a pair."
Molly said, "*Snowdrop*—it's a flower."
Sue said, "*Snowflake*."
"What about *snowball*?" Chris asked.
Roger said, "This snow makes great snowballs."
"I can make a perfect snowball," Sam added.
"I can too," Molly said.
"Me too," said Chris.
"Me too," said Sue.
So that's how everyone started to make snowballs.
At first, everyone just wanted to make
a perfect snowball.
Perfectly round.
Perfectly packed.
Perfectly white.

Roger put his snowballs in a row in front of him.

He made a row of four.

On top he put a row of three.

Then two.

Then one.

Everybody copied Roger.

Soon there were ten snowballs piled

in front of everyone.

"These look like cannonballs," Scott said.

"Yeah. They do," said Chris. "Like the
        cannonballs I saw when my grandpa took me
        to see an old battlefield."

"Where was it?" Molly asked.

"I think it was in Pennsylvania," Chris answered.

"Are there still cannonballs?"

"Don't think so," Chris said.

Who threw the first snowball?
Nobody knew.
But one snowball led to
another snowball . . .

and another . . . and another . . .
and another.

Before they knew it, the *Small Potatoes*
were having a snowball fight!

"Gotcha!" yelled Sue.

"Gotcha back!" yelled Scott.

"I'm going to get you this time!" Sam shouted.
"Watch out!" Roger screamed back.

All of a sudden there was quiet.

Molly lay on the ground.

Blood was dripping down one cheek.

Chris had thrown a snowball.

It must have had a chunk of ice inside.

Molly's cheek was bleeding a lot.

Just under her eye.

Chris felt awful.

He hadn't meant to hurt Molly.

He hadn't meant to make her cry.

Spot tried to make Molly feel better,

but his licks didn't seem to help.

"I think we'd better walk Molly home,"
    said Sue.

"Maybe she needs stitches."

"Or maybe just a Band-Aid."

"Let's go!" said Sue.

CHAPTER FOUR

MOLLY'S HURT

Chris rang Molly's doorbell.

"Molly's hurt," he said to her mother. "It was
an accident. I hit her on the cheek with an
icy snowball."

37

Molly's mother took Molly inside and
shut the door.

Spot scooted inside just before the door closed.

Roger, Sue, Chris, Sam, and Scott
waited in the front hall.

They were scared—especially Chris.

Roger remembered how much his lip had
bled once when he had cut it.

"It bled all over my shirt," he said.

"Blood tastes yucky," Sam said.

"My mom says it usually looks worse
       than it is," Scott said.

"I hope your mom is right," Chris said.

"Mostly, she is," Scott answered.

Just then Molly opened the door.

She had a Band-Aid on her cheek.

A small one.

"I'm fine," she said. "It's only a
    small cut."

"I'm glad," Chris said. "And I'm glad
    you don't need stitches."

"Me too," said Molly. "Want some
    hot chocolate?"

40

Molly invited everyone inside.

They had to take off their boots,

and snow pants, and snow jackets,

and mittens, and hats, and scarves.

But for hot chocolate, it was worth it.

Molly put a plateful of doughnuts on the table.

Spot stayed close to Molly and whined.

He wanted food.

"I'll give you the hole," Sam said to Spot.

"You can have mine too," Sue said.

Spot didn't think Sam and Sue were funny.

He didn't want the hole, he wanted the doughnut.

He wanted something real to eat!

Chris felt sorry for Spot and shared his doughnut.

When Spot begged for more, Molly said, "No more!
    You'll get sick."

Spot knew Molly meant it.

He walked away from the table and headed
for his bowl.

A bowlful of water would wash down the doughnut.

Gulp! Gulp!

Splash!

"What should we do now?" Roger asked.

"We can go back outside," said Sue.

"And do what?"

"Do something fun—like make snow angels."

"Or build a snowman."

"But that means we have to get all dressed
     again," moaned Scott.

"So what!" Sam said.

"Yeah. It's not so hard," added Chris.

"What do we need for the snowman?"
     Sam asked.

There were lots of ideas.

A broom. A carrot.

A scarf and a hat.

Something for eyes—maybe apples or cookies.

Roger said, "Once I made a super snowman who
     wore eyeglasses."

"Where'd you get them?" Molly asked.

"I had an old pair," answered Roger.

"I'll ask my mom if she has some old glasses,"
     said Molly.

"Why are we just making a snowman?" Sue asked.

"We should make a snowlady too."

"I agree," Molly said.

"It's okay with me," Roger said.

"Ditto," Chris said.

"There's a good straw hat in the basement," said
       Molly. "I'll ask if we can use it."

"But no apron!" Sue said. "All snowladies wear
       aprons. Let's make ours different."

"How?" Sam asked.

"Maybe we could find a coat," Scott suggested.

"And maybe an umbrella."

"Good idea—if it starts to snow, she won't
       lose her shape!" Sue said.

"And if it rains?"

"She'll melt anyway—but slowly!"
       Sue said, laughing at her own joke.

"So let's get dressed."

"Hurry up, Scott! You're very slow.

   And the last one outside is a rotten egg!"

CHAPTER FIVE

IT'S SNOWING AGAIN!

Suc was the first one outside.

She lay down on her back.

She put her hands at her sides.

Slowly she spread her arms.

When she couldn't reach any higher,

she stood up—carefully.

"Look what I made," Sue shouted.

"A snow angel!"

"It's snowing again," said Roger.

"We'd better work fast."

"Right," said Molly. "When it starts
to snow hard, my mom will make me
and Spot go inside."

"So let's work together," Roger said.

"I'll work with you. Chris, who
do you want for a partner?"

Chris picked Sam.

So Sue got Scott.

49

Roger and Molly made a big snowball—
as big as they could get it.
Then they began to roll it around the yard.
The more they rolled, the bigger it got.
"If we roll this just a little more," said
Roger, "it will be a good bottom."
"For the snowman?" Molly asked.
"Or the snowlady," said Roger. "It doesn't
matter. But it's not big enough yet."
Roger pushed.
Molly pushed.
Spot pushed too.
"I can't push anymore," said Molly. "Isn't this
big enough?"
"Almost. Just one more time around the yard."

Roger and Molly were finished.

Their ball was so big they could not push it anymore—not one more inch.

"Can we put ours on top?" Chris asked.

"No, not yours," Sue said. "Take ours next. It's bigger."

Roger checked both balls.

He decided Sue's was bigger, so it should be in the middle.

"Everybody help," said Molly. "This is heavy." And it was.

But somehow, they managed to put it on top of Roger and Molly's base.

Molly packed some snow around the bottom so it wouldn't fall off.

53

"Now can we put ours on top?" Chris asked.

"Sure," said Molly.

"It's a perfect head," Sam said.

"But it needs eyes, a nose, and a mouth,"
Chris reminded the others.

"You're right," said Roger. "I'll get the stuff."

There was a lot of arguing about the
snowman's face.

Should it have cookie eyes and a carrot nose?

Or carrot eyes and a cookie nose?

And what about the mouth?

Should it be a sliced apple? A row of raisins?

Finally, everyone agreed on just the right features.

And the snowman was finished.

Look over there!

You can see what it looked like.

The snowlady went fast.

Because of good teamwork.

And because everybody knew exactly
what to do.

She was smaller than the snowman—
but just a little.

"She looks different than other snowladies,"
        said Sam.

"She's all dressed up!" Molly exclaimed.

"She looks like she's ready to go to work,"
        Roger said.

"Just like my mom!" Scott added.

"And mine!" said Sue.

"My hands are freezing," said Roger.

"Mine too," said Scott. "We can't just stand
around admiring what we made."

"But it's good!" Molly said.

"But it's too cold!" said Scott. "I'm going home."

"But when's our next meeting?" asked Sam.

"When it's warmer," Scott said as he left.

"Wait a minute," said Roger. "Why don't we have
a meeting the next time it snows?"

"Good idea," said Molly.

"Bow wow," said Spot, wagging his tail.

So the next meeting of the *Small Potatoes Club*
is the next time it snows.

Hope you can come.

And bring your membership card.

"See you next meeting!"

SMALL POTATOES FUN

- Try color mixing. Use paints, or food coloring, or Kool-Aid, just like Molly. Whatever you use, have fun!
- Since you are now a member of the *Small Potatoes Club*, make a membership card for yourself. You can copy the one below or invent your own.